Fairy Tale Kingdom

Rapunzel's Tower

Cinderella's House

Enchanted Tree

Fairy Godmother's House

Prince Charming's Castle

Seven Dwarfs' House

Sleeping Beauty's Castle

Clock Tower

Celeste's House

Verity's House

Wicked Queen's Castle

Chapter One
Verity's Task

All the fairies gathered around the enchanted tree by the light of the full moon. They worked hard to keep everyone happy and safe in the Fairy Tale Kingdom. Tonight, the fairy who had worked the hardest would be announced. Tatiana, the Queen of the Fairies, would present the winner with a beautiful sparkly star.

Verity stood next
to her best friend, Celeste,
as they waited. The two
fairies loved spending time
together. They liked
baking fairy cakes,
playing games, and reading
their favourite magazine, *Sparkle Time*.

"Please let it be me, please let it be me."
Verity crossed her fingers tightly.

"I think it will be Fay," whispered Celeste.
She tucked a lock of her dark-brown hair
behind her ear. "She's been working non-stop!"

"Oh, pickled pumpkins!" grumbled
Verity.

"And the winner is... Fay!" Tatiana
announced happily.

Everyone clapped. Fay stood up and proudly opened the magical box. All the fairies gazed with wonder. A sparkly orange star floated high into the sky and then came back down to land in Fay's hands.

"Phew, I thought she was going to get a lilac star," chuckled Verity. She tried to hide her disappointment. "I've already got an orange star," she boasted. "I want to be the first fairy to get a lilac star!"

Verity worried that she didn't win stars as often as the other fairies. She liked to tell the truth ALL the time, which of course is a good thing, but it could cause problems. Luckily, Celeste was always there to help. Sometimes Verity would surprise herself and save the day. She just wished it would happen more often.

"It doesn't matter what colour the star is," Celeste said kindly. She offered Verity her favourite sweet, a marshmallow, to cheer her up.

"It does when you want to have all the colours of the rainbow. Also, lilac is the **rarest**. Everyone wants a lilac star," said Verity. She popped the marshmallow into her mouth. She was determined to try harder with the next task she was given.

"That's true," agreed Celeste. "It looks like Tatiana is calling you over. This might be your chance to earn another star. Good luck!" Celeste's big brown eyes sparkled with excitement.

Verity waited as Tatiana removed her golden cloak. It matched her shiny long golden hair. Verity twiddled her pink hair and wondered what the task would be. She hoped it wouldn't be too difficult. She really wanted to do well this time.

rarest Most unusual

Tatiana smiled. "Verity, I would like you
to be the voice of the Wicked Queen's magic
mirror. You must do everything you can to
protect Snow White, her lovely step-daughter.
Remember Verity, the Queen is very wicked,
so you have to be careful!" said Tatiana.

"How can I protect Snow White when I'm in a mirror?" Verity asked.

"You must answer the Wicked Queen's questions and tell her whatever she wants to hear. If you don't, she will become very cross and will be mean to Snow White. It is our duty, as fairies, to keep everyone happy and safe in the Fairy Tale Kingdom. Do you understand?" Tatiana raised an eyebrow at Verity.

Verity was worried. What if she accidentally blurted out the truth? But she really wanted to help Snow White. She screwed up her nose and nodded **reluctantly**. "I understand," she said.

reluctantly   Without really wanting to

Chapter Two
Verity Gets to Work

As Verity approached the Wicked Queen's castle, dark clouds **hovered** in the sky above and two huge stone vultures guarded the entrance. Verity thought it looked very gloomy, but then she noticed the sun shining down like a spotlight on one area of the garden. Animals had gathered around a girl with curly hair and kind eyes. A soft, grey

hovered Floated on the spot

rabbit was sitting in her lap while she fed
a hungry fox an apple from her hand,
and squirrels playfully chased each other
around her feet.

"Wow, that must be Snow White!" Verity said to herself.

"I'm Verity," Verity announced as she approached Snow White. "Tatiana, the Queen of the Fairies sent me. I'm a fairy, by the way." Verity pulled out her wand and showed it to Snow White as proof.

"Oh, it's so nice to meet you!" Snow White hugged Verity. "I like your hair – pink is my favourite colour."

"Oh, um, thank you," faltered Verity. She could see why the animals liked Snow White, she was so friendly and kind.

A fearful shriek came from inside the castle. "Why isn't my magic mirror talking to me?" boomed the voice.

"That's the Queen!" Snow White said in a panic. "You mustn't get in her way. She can be very mean."

"Don't worry," Verity said confidently. "I'm here to protect you now."

"Really?" Snow White's emerald-green eyes sparkled. "How are you going to do that?"

"I'm going to be the voice of the Wicked Queen's magic mirror," Verity said proudly. She stood up straight and pushed back her shoulders.

"Right. OK. I think you need to fly inside and do that now!" said Snow White anxiously.

"Oops!" Verity felt flustered.

"Take these berries in case you get hungry." The ever-thoughtful Snow White handed Verity a small basket. "Good luck!"

Verity looked at the map of the castle that Tatiana had given her. She could see the Wicked Queen's large bedroom window at the top and she quickly flew inside. There was the large, gold-framed magic mirror. She squeezed through a small gap between the frame and the glass itself. Once she was behind the glass,

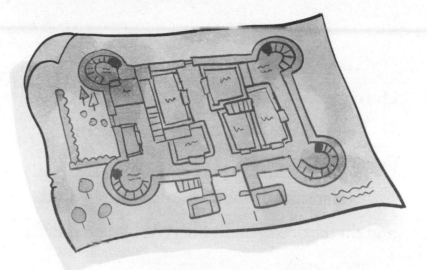

she found a little stool to sit on. She took a
deep breath to calm her racing heart. Then
she unpacked her magazine, *Sparkle Time*. She
took it wherever she went, just in case she had
time to read it.

She popped a juicy berry into her
mouth and looked around. Just then, the
Wicked Queen pressed her face up against
the outside of the mirror. Her pointy nose
and **beady** eyes seemed very close to Verity.

---

beady   Small, round, and bright

The Wicked Queen placed both hands on the gold frame.

"Mirror, mirror on the wall, who is the loveliest of them all?" she screeched.

Her voice was so loud that Verity fell off the stool. She spilled her berries and dropped her magazine.

"Umm, I believe it's Snow White?" Verity blurted out without thinking. She had completely forgotten her instructions to keep the Wicked Queen happy.

"SNOW WHITE! Why is SHE the loveliest?" demanded the Queen.

"Well, she's very kind," Verity replied **swiftly**. She felt a little calmer now. "She's actually in my magazine, *Sparkle Time*, this week because she's just opened a squirrel

hospital. Would you like to have a look at what it says?"

The Wicked Queen furiously turned away from the mirror and ordered her huntsman to find Snow White. "Take her to the forest and kill her. Then bring me her heart as proof!"

A deathly silence fell throughout the palace. In the forest, the birds had stopped singing and the sun hid behind the clouds. The **eerie** silence was broken by a tiny sound.

"Uh-oh!" squeaked the mirror.

eerie   Strange and frightening

23

Chapter Three
Celeste to the Rescue

There was only one way out of this and that was to call for the fairy who always helped Verity – her best friend, Celeste.

"Celeste! Celeste!" cried Verity. "Please can you come quickly? I need your help!"

Within a flash, Celeste was by Verity's side.

"What's happened?" Celeste asked **cautiously**.

cautiously   Very carefully

"The Wicked Queen has ordered Snow White to be killed!" Verity's big brown eyes were wide with fear.

Celeste gasped and put her hand to her mouth. "Why?"

"Well, she asked the mirror who was the loveliest and I accidentally told her it was Snow White!"

"Oh Verity!" cried Celeste. "Come on, we need to put this right!"

Celeste and Verity flew as fast as they could and caught up with the huntsman who had been ordered to kill Snow White.

"Right, I'll talk to the huntsman. You fly down to the butchers, buy an animal heart and bring it back," Celeste told Verity.

"I don't think now is a good time to go shopping!" replied Verity.

Celeste sighed. "It's so the huntsman can take it to the Queen and pretend it's Snow White's heart!"

"Oh," nodded Verity. "Umm, that's lying..."

Celeste raised an eyebrow. "Just hurry up!" she cried.

When Verity returned with the animal heart, Celeste had managed to convince the huntsman to help them.

"All we need to do now is hide Snow White. Then she'll be safe!" said Verity happily.

But Celeste had a feeling it wouldn't be that easy.

Chapter Four
A Trip to the Forest

Verity and Celeste stood in the middle of the forest with Snow White. The sunlight shone through the leaves on the trees down to the ground. The birds were singing loudly and the whole forest had a delightful fresh smell of pine.

"It's very nice of you both to bring me on a day trip to the forest." Snow White sighed happily.

Verity and Celeste looked at each other. "Actually, it's not a day trip," Verity said quietly.

"We just thought it best if you were out of the Wicked Queen's way for a while," continued Celeste. "You know, sometimes she can be a bit..."

Verity made a face like an angry lion. Snow White laughed. "You two are the nicest fairies I have ever met!"

"You're right, Verity," Celeste whispered. "She's wonderful! It's such a shame we have to hide her away. We need to make sure she is never found by the Queen."

Suddenly seven dwarfs walked past in a line. They marched into a small, pretty white cottage with yellow roses growing around the front door and dark-framed windows.

"I've got it!" Verity shouted happily. "Snow White could live with them. No one would ever find her there."

Verity knocked loudly on the dwarfs' door.

"What do you want?" growled a dwarf.

"I was just wondering if you had room for my friend to stay? She's very kind and helpful..." but before Verity could finish, the dwarf slammed the door shut.

Verity was shocked. She knocked again. This time the door was opened very slowly by another dwarf, who peeked out.

"Hello," said Verity, but before she could say anything else the dwarf's face turned bright red and he quickly shut the door.

Verity was starting to get frustrated. She knocked on the door again. Another dwarf opened the door. "Hello," said Verity. "What's your name?"

The dwarf shrugged. "I don't know!" he said and walked out of the house, slamming the door behind him.

"Where are you going?" shouted Verity.

"I don't know!" replied the dwarf as he walked into a tree.

Verity knocked on the door AGAIN. The door opened. "Are you still here?" asked the first dwarf.

Before Verity could reply, Snow White

suddenly appeared right next to her.

"Oh dear, have you had a bad day?"
Snow White asked the dwarf gently. "Why
don't I make you a hot chocolate and you can
tell me all about it?" And to Verity's surprise,
the dwarf smiled and invited Snow White in.

A little later, Verity left the dwarfs'
cottage and walked back to Celeste, shaking
her head in disbelief. "All the dwarfs were
happy to have Snow White live with them.
They absolutely love her!" Verity told Celeste.

Celeste lightly clapped her hands.
"That's great!"

"I'm not sure why she likes them so much.
Their house is very messy, and they didn't offer
me a single marshmallow!" complained Verity.

"You sound as cross as the first dwarf," giggled Celeste.

*

Back at the Wicked Queen's castle, Verity and Celeste looked up at the large grey **turrets**.

"Verity, you need to go back inside the mirror. Do you think you can remember what to say to the Wicked Queen when she asks the mirror who is the loveliest?" asked Celeste.

"Yesssssss!" replied Verity. "But..."

"What?" replied Celeste impatiently.

"What if I say the wrong thing again?"

"Verity, I know it's important to tell the truth. But sometimes, especially if it puts someone in danger, it's best not to say anything at all," Celeste said kindly.

---

turrets Narrow towers

Verity thought for a moment. "That would be very boring. I like talking and I really like helping people. After all, isn't that what fairies do, help people?"

Celeste smiled and gave Verity a big hug. "Snow White is relying on you. You can do this, Verity."

Chapter Five
Brave Verity

A few days later, Verity had fallen fast asleep inside the Wicked Queen's mirror. She was having a wonderful dream about being just like Snow White. But instead of being surrounded by animals, Verity was surrounded by marshmallows. Suddenly, a booming voice woke her up and she fell off her stool for the third time that day.

"WHO IS THE LOVELIEST OF THEM ALL?" demanded the Wicked Queen.

Verity was so confused; she didn't know where she was or what she was supposed to be doing. "Snow White," mumbled Verity, half-asleep.

"Snow White is dead!" replied the Wicked Queen angrily.

"No she's not!" replied Verity, yawning and rubbing her eyes. "She's living in the forest with the seven dwarfs."

"What?" roared the Wicked Queen. "Well, not for much longer!" she hissed **viciously**. "I'll make sure that she's never the loveliest ever again!"

viciously   Violently and cruelly

She began to
disguise herself as an
old lady. "Snow White
won't be able to resist a
juicy apple. Even if it is
covered with poison,"
the Wicked Queen
cackled loudly.

Verity suddenly remembered
where she was. Then she realized what she
had just said. And then it dawned on her
what the Wicked Queen was planning to do
to Snow White!

On the table next to the window, Verity
spotted a shiny red apple and a little bottle
of poison. If only she could get close enough
to wave her magic wand over the bottle.

cackled   Laughed unpleasantly

Verity's heart was pounding. She carefully sneaked out from behind the mirror while the Wicked Queen was adjusting her wig.

Verity was so scared that she thought her wings might stop working. But she was determined to save Snow White. She took a deep breath and remembered Celeste's words: "You can do this, Verity." She waved her wand at lightning speed over the poison. Then she flew even faster back behind the mirror.

She only hoped that she had tu**rned** the poison into a potion of Delightful Dreams in time. Verity peeped out of the side of the mirror again. At the same moment, the Wicked Queen slammed the door shut behind her.

Verity could see that the little bottle was empty and the basket of red shiny apples had gone.

Meanwhile, Celeste was at home busily baking fairy cakes. She really hoped that Verity was staying out of trouble.

Suddenly Tatiana flew down at a terrific speed, bringing with her an air of panic.

"Snow White is dead!" she cried.

A huge gasp rippled across the Fairy Tale Kingdom.

"What happened?" asked Celeste.

"The Wicked Queen dressed up as an old woman. She poisoned an apple, which she handed to Snow White," replied Tatiana, breathlessly.

As quick as a flash, Celeste flew off. Something told her that Verity might, just might, have said the wrong thing.

Fireworks were being let off as Celeste approached the castle of the Wicked Queen. In an attic room at the top of the castle was a fairy with her nose pressed against the window. Her face was full of gloom.

Celeste's heart sank.

She entered the dark and dusty attic room. She could hear Verity's sad little expressionless voice watching the fireworks light up the dark sky.

"Ooh... ahhh!" Verity loved watching fireworks. But Celeste could tell Verity's mind was very far away, lost in sadness.

"Verity, are you ok?"

"Fireworks... pretty..." whispered Verity without moving. Her face was still pressed against the window.

Celeste put her arm around Verity. "Do you want to tell me what happened?" she asked.

Verity shook her head and a single tear rolled down her cheek.

"Verity, if you tell me what happened we might be able to fix it?" said Celeste gently.

"I tried to save Snow White by turning the bottle of poison into Delightful Dreams. But it didn't work because now Snow White won't wake up!" Verity started to cry.

Celeste winced. "Verity, please don't cry."

"I... can't... help... it!" sobbed Verity. "It's all my fault!"

Chapter Six
A Prince Visits

Suddenly, Celeste realized something. "Verity, how many drops of the potion did the Wicked Queen put on the apple?"

"I didn't see." Verity dabbed her eyes and sniffed. "But the bottle is empty, so I think she used it all."

"Yes!" said Celeste bouncing on her toes. "Snow White isn't dead – she's in a deep sleep!

You're only supposed to use a few drops of Delightful Dreams, not the whole bottle! And now there's only one way to wake her up... remember?"

Verity looked blankly at Celeste.

"With a kiss from a handsome prince, of course!" Celeste smiled.

Verity didn't smile. "I'm not dressing up again!" she said. "I did enough of that when I had to pretend to be the wolf for Little Red Riding Hood!"

Celeste laughed. "I'm not asking you to dress up. But I do happen to know that a certain Prince is in town at the moment!"

"Not Prince Charming?" Verity said excitedly. "I LOVE him! Can I ask him for his **autograph**?"

---

autograph   Signature of someone famous

"Or we could ask him to kiss Snow White?" suggested Celeste.

"Ooh can I be the one to ask him? Please, please, please," Verity pleaded excitedly.

So, Celeste and Verity found Prince Charming and took him to Snow White's

bedside. Verity crossed her fingers tightly. She really hoped this would work.

When the Prince kissed Snow White, she opened her eyes, stretched and sat up. Verity was so happy that she jumped up and punched the air for joy.

"Verity, you saved me from the Wicked Queen," Snow White said happily. "I knew you could do it!"

Verity hung her head and looked sadly at her sparkly boots. "Actually, I accidentally told the Wicked Queen you were living with the seven dwarfs. I'm so sorry." Verity quickly told Snow White the whole story. She was sure that Snow White would be cross.

"Verity, you saved me." Snow White said kindly. "You swapped the poison for Delightful Dreams. Without your quick thinking, I wouldn't be here now."

"Thank you," Verity said quietly.

"Wow, she really is the kindest person EVER!" Celeste whispered to Verity.

Chapter Seven
Verity's Sparkly Star

Celeste was surprised that Verity wasn't at the seven dwarfs' party for Snow White. She was even more surprised when she found Verity visiting the Wicked Queen.

She could hear Verity's voice from inside the magic mirror.

"...So you see, it's not looks that make you beautiful. It's about how you treat others,"

Verity told the Wicked Queen. "That's real beauty!"

Celeste winced. She was sure the Wicked Queen was going to shout. Or worse still, throw something at the mirror.

"Thank you Magic Mirror. You've given me some great ideas!" said the Wicked Queen nicely.

Celeste couldn't believe it!

A few days later, Verity went to buy the latest copy of *Sparkle Time* magazine. The shop was really busy. Verity could hear a familiar voice speaking to the crowd. "My new book tells you how to feel great about yourself."

Verity managed to squeeze past everyone to get to the front. The Wicked Queen was

holding up a copy of
her new book, *Kindness
is Beautiful*.

"As you all know,"
continued the Wicked
Queen. "I used to be
very mean and I always
wanted to be the most
beautiful. But then I realized something.
If you're a nice person on the inside, then
you're beautiful on the outside."

Everyone in the shop cheered and clapped.
Verity was very proud. She knew that she had
helped the Wicked Queen change.

*

Once again, all the fairies had gathered
around the enchanted tree by the light of the

full moon. Tatiana looked very pleased.

"I'm extremely proud to present this extra-special star to a fairy who risked everything to save Snow White." Tatiana handed the magic box to Verity. "Well done, Verity."

"Thank you very much," beamed Verity, she crossed her fingers and held her breath. She really wanted the lilac star.

As she opened the box, a beautiful rainbow star floated out. All the fairies gasped. They had never seen a rainbow star before. Everyone cheered and clapped for Verity.

"Rainbow stars are given out very rarely," Tatiana explained.

"Wow, that's amazing, Verity." Celeste hugged her friend. "You really deserve it."

"Thank you, Celeste," said Verity quietly. "I couldn't have done any of this without you."

Celeste smiled. "Ooh your rainbow star has lilac in it. You don't need a lilac star now."

Verity frowned. "Celeste, I've already told you! I want to be the first fairy to get a fully lilac star."

Celeste chuckled. "You're one of a kind, Verity!"

Fairy Quiz

1 Which fairy has pink hair?

2 Who is Verity's best friend?

3 Which fairy won the sparkly orange star at the beginning?

4 What did Snow White give Verity to take with her in case she became hungry?

5 What did the Wicked Queen put on the apple that she handed to Snow White?

6 What colour are the roses on the outside of the seven dwarfs' house?

7 How many dwarfs are there?

8 What is the title of the Wicked Queen's book?

Answers

1. Verity 2. Celeste 3. Fay 4. Berries 5. Poison
6. Yellow 7. Seven 8. *Kindness is Beautiful*

DK | Penguin Random House

Illustrations by Amy Zhing
Designed by Collaborate Agency
Fiction editor Heather Featherstone
Educational consultants Jacqueline Harris, Jenny Lane-Smith

Senior editors Amy Braddon, Marie Greenwood
Senior designer Ann Cannings
Managing editor Laura Gilbert
Managing art editor Diane Peyton Jones
Production editor Dragana Puvacic
Production controller Francesca Sturiale
Publishing manager Francesca Young

First published in Great Britain in 2021 by
Dorling Kindersley Limited
DK, One Embassy Gardens, 8 Viaduct Gardens,
London, SW11 7BW

The authorised representative in the EEA is
Dorling Kindersley Verlag GmbH. Arnulfstr. 124,
80636 Munich, Germany

A CIP catalogue record for this book
is available from the British Library.
ISBN: 9-780-2415-0345-4

Printed and bound in Great Britain by
Clays Ltd, Elcograf S.p.A.

For the curious
www.dk.com